Archie's Fun 'N' Games Activity Book

Published by Archie Comic Publications, Inc.
325 Fayette Avenue, Mamaroneck, NY 10543-2318.

ISBN: 978-1-936975-51-8

Printed in USA.

PUBLISHER/CO-CEO: Jon Goldwater
CO-CEO: Nancy Silberkleit
PRESIDENT: Mike Pellerito
CO-PRESIDENT/EDITOR-IN-CHIEF: Victor Gorelick
CFO: William Mooar
SENIOR VICE PRESIDENT, SALES & BUSINESS DEVELOPMENT:
Jim Sokolowski
SENIOR VICE PRESIDENT, PUBLISHING & OPERATIONS:
Harold Buchholz
VICE PRESIDENT, SPECIAL PROJECTS:
Steve Mooar
EXECUTIVE DIRECTOR OF EDITORIAL:
Paul Kaminski
PRODUCTION MANAGER:
Stephen Oswald
DIRECTOR OF PUBLICITY & MARKETING: Steven Scott
PROJECT COORDINATOR/BOOK DESIGN: Duncan McLachlan
EDITORIAL ASSISTANT/PROOFREADER: Jonathan Mosley

This book was made possible by the puzzling talents of these writers and artists:

Now the fun begins! Just turn the page and start!

Veronica BIRD FIND!

WHAT DOES VERONICA SEE?! LOOK FOR THE BIRD NAMES IN THE BIRD FIND! YOU'LL HAVE TO LOOK UP, DOWN, FORWARD, BACKWARD AND DIAGONALLY! THEN, CHECK OFF WHAT YOU'VE FOUND ON THE BIRD LIST BELOW!!

```
N E R W C R E K C E P D O O W
R O E V S O S K T B E R I S E
S P A R R O W R E H L D B A G
        A R O A G L P D
        L C S G S U S R
          N O E U I
          I V J C B
        R T E A K E
        T H H Y E U
        B G E E R L
        R I G D S B
        I N I B O R
```

OFFICIAL BIRD LIST:
ROBIN · WOODPECKER · SPARROW
LARK · NIGHTINGALE · WREN
BLUEJAY · SAPSUCKER · BLUEBIRD

DILTON IN A BONE TO PICK!

DILTON'S PUT TOGETHER A DINOSAUR SKELETON IN HIS LAB, BUT HE HAS ONE BONE LEFT OVER! FILL IN THE ANSWERS TO THE QUESTIONS BELOW TO FIND OUT WHAT TYPE OF BONE IT IS!

1. DAY _ _ THE DINOSAURS.
2. _ _ _ _-BILLED DINOSAURS.
3. THE FLINTSTONES' PET'S NAME.
4. A SINGING PURPLE DINOSAUR.
5. PTERODACTYLS WERE _ _ _ _ _ _ _ DINOSAURS.
6. STUDYING DINOSAURS IS DILTON'S _ _ _ _ _ .
7. TRICERATOPS HAD THREE _ _ _ _ _ .
8. WE LEARN ABOUT DINOSAURS FROM THEIR _ _ _ _ _ .
9. TYRANNOSAURUS _ _ _ .

1. OF 2. DUCK 3. DINO 4. BARNEY 5. FLYING 6. HOBBY 7. HORNS 8. BONES 9. REX

REGGIE THE EGO TRIPPER!

EGOTISTICAL REGGIE HAS SOME THOUGHTS RUNNING AROUND HIS HEAD. TO FIND OUT WHAT THEY ARE —TRACE THE PATH THROUGH HIS HEAD AND WRITE DOWN EACH LETTER AS YOU COME TO IT FOR THE MESSAGE! START HERE

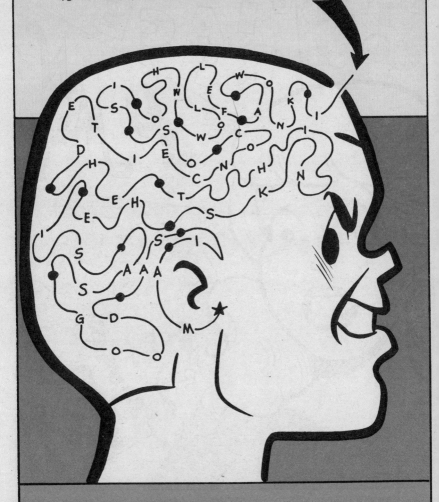

HEY! LET'S EAT! FIND THE FOOD ITEMS IN THE WORD SEARCH! LOOK UP, DOWN, FORWARDS, BACK-WARDS, AND DIAGONALLY! CROSS THEM OFF THE LIST BELOW AS YOU FIND THEM! --CHOW DOWN!!

Jughead

U S R E G R U B M A H
B R O C C O L I M T C
N E K C I H C A A O I
H D E A W
O P R G D
W F C O N
M S E D A
E R C T S
I L I O R
N O P H R
S T O P O
E T M A

FOOD LIST:
APPLE
SANDWICH
BROCCOLI
CHOW MEIN
CHICKEN
HAMBURGER
ICE CREAM
HOT DOG

Archie in
BROKE AGAIN!
UNSCRAMBLE THE WORDS BELOW TO FIND OUT WHAT ARCHIE NEEDS! ANSWERS BELOW!
WHAT'S THE STORY?
1 YENOM
2 GUDHO
3 LOAOM
4 SHAC
R
The ANSWERS!
1. MONEY 2. DOUGH
3. MOOLA 4. CASH

MISTER LODGE

WHO'S THE BANE OF MY EXISTANCE? --THAT'S RIGHT... **ARCHIE!** SEE HOW MANY TIMES YOU CAN FIND THE MENACE'S NAME IN THE WORD SEARCH! LOOK UP, DOWN, FORWARD, BACKWARD, AND DIAGONALLY! THE ANSWER IS GIVEN BELOW!

```
H A R C H I E C
C R E I H C R A
E C R A E E H I R
I H H I I I C E A
H I C H R H R I
C E C A E C A H
R R I H C R E C
A I E A R A I R
R H C R A H C A
C A R C H I E R
H A E I H C R A
I E I H C R A
E E H A I H C
E E C R E E R
I I R C I A
H H A H H
C C C I C
R R A E R
A A R C A
```

THE ANSWER: "SEVENTEEN"

YOU'VE GOT TO HELP ME! I JUST FINISHED SHOPPING AT THE NEW RIVERDALE 27-ACRE MEGA-MALL AND I CAN'T FIND MY CAR! --YIPE!!
Archie
START HERE:
NO WAY!
YOU'RE LOST!
GO BACK, DUDE!
FORGET IT!
DEAD END!
YOU'VE FOUND THE CAR!!

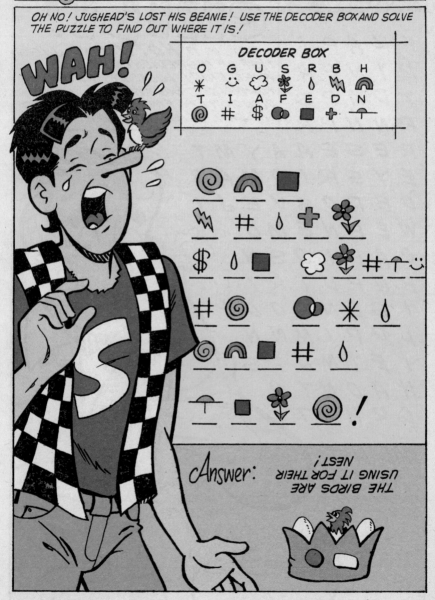

CHUCK CLAYTON AMATEUR BOXER!

P	G	N	I	R	I	
L	L	T	P	O	P	
E	O	R	U	U	F	T
E	V	U	N	N	I	A
R	E	N	C	D	G	T
E	S	K	H	C	H	T
F	I	S	L	T	T	E
E	K	O	O	H	R	S
R	J	A	B	G	T	O
T	I	L	P	I	Y	C
U	G	G	E	E	E	L
O	N	C	S	W	S	R
K	I	R	N	Y	N	E
C	T	O	E	V	E	N
O	T	S	F	A	F	R
N	R	S	E	E	F	O
K	P	A	D	H	O	C

BOXING WORD LIST:

GLOVES
TRUNKS
KNOCKOUT
CORNER
PUNCH
FIGHT
REFEREE
HEAVY-WEIGHT
OFFENSE
DEFENCE
FOULS
HOOK
CROSS
JAB

ANSWER: "DO NOT PASS ALGEBRA ... DO NOT COLLECT DIPLOMA!!"

Sabrina ✱ DO YOU BELIEVE IN MAGIC?✱

*F*IND THE WORDS RELATED TO A MAGIC SHOW IN THE FOLLOWING WORD FIND!!

```
L W A N D Y R
T Y B V P V H
Y N R Q J L A
I R A B B I T
M S C I M V L
T P A V A P I
X E D O G S N
L L A T I J T
Y L B L C O J
P S R Y I T S
J R A Z A P A
F P Y Q N Z P
```

Word List:

SPELLS, ZAP, MAGICIAN, HAT, RABBIT, WAND, ABRACADABRA ✱☆✱

Jughead • FUNNY people •

TRY TO MATCH UP THESE FUNNY PEOPLE
TO THEIR APPROPRIATE PLACES!

1	CLOWN	A	COMEDY CLUB
2	CARTOON CHARACTER	B	KING'S CASTLE
3	COURT JESTER	C	CIRCUS
4	COMEDIAN	D	DECK OF CARDS
5	JOKER	E	COMIC BOOK

ANSWERS:
1-C   2-E   3-B   4-A   5-D

Archie in CRYING FOUL!

ARCHIE'S BEEN EATING SOME PRETTY NASTY STUFF, AND VERONICA'S PAYING THE PRICE! FIND ALL THE ITEMS IN THE WORD SEARCH BELOW!

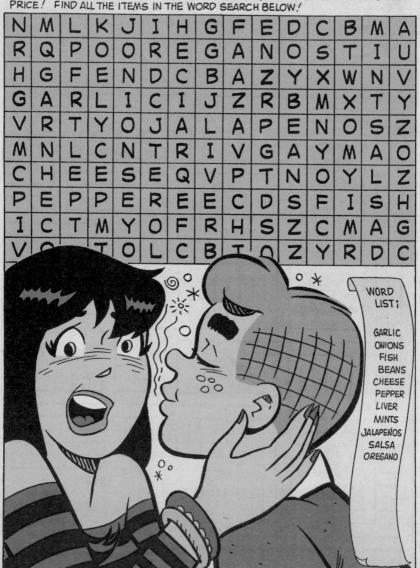

WORD LIST:

GARLIC
ONIONS
FISH
BEANS
CHEESE
PEPPER
LIVER
MINTS
JALAPEÑOS
SALSA
OREGANO

Veronica

IN

Fill in the Blanks!

Help Veronica finish up her new crossword outfit by filling in all those blanks! Good luck!

ACROSS

1. MARILYN MONROE'S INITIALS.
3. STYLISH
5. VERONICA LIKES TO SPEND THIS.
6. SWEET FOOD.
7. ___ BRADY BUNCH.
8. THE GROUP THAT GOES AFTER THE BAD GUY IN A WESTERN.

DOWN

2. THE SHORT INHABITANTS OF THE LAND OF OZ.
3. HORSES EAT THIS.
4. A FAVORITE MOVIE FOOD.
6. OPPOSITE OF HOT.
8. JOSIE AND THE _____ .
9. BILL AND TED'S _____ ADVENTURE.

The ANSWERS: ACROSS - ① MM ③ HIP ⑤ MONEY ⑥ CANDY ⑦ THE ⑧ POSSE DOWN ② MUNCHKINS ③ HAY ④ POPCORN ⑥ COLD ⑧ PUSSYCATS ⑨ EXCELLENT

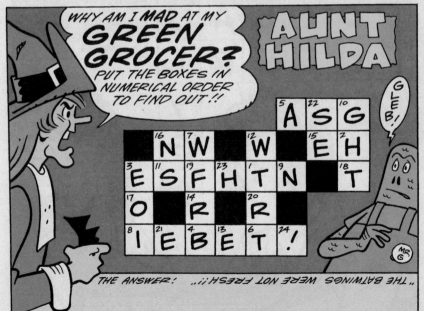

HEY, Jug!

THIS PUZZLE IS JUST FOR YOU, BECAUSE ALL THE ANSWERS HAVE SOMETHING TO DO WITH FOOD!

ACROSS

1. THE "T" IN A BLT

4. --- CORN

6. ------ CREAM PIE

7. TWO PEAS IN A ---

8. YOU CAN TUNE A PIANO BUT YOU CAN'T ---- FISH

DOWN

1. POPULAR MEXICAN FOOD

2. WHAT YOU PUT ON A HOT DOG

3. CARBONATED BEVERAGE

5. ---- AND PEPPER

ACROSS 1. TOMATO 4. POP 6. BANANA 7. POD 8. TUNA
DOWN 1. TACO 3. MUSTARD 3. SODA 5. SALT

Veronica FITNESS FIND!!

```
S A N K T I G N C L O E A J O B
W E I G H T S T A N T E H S O I
I N C S H W U D O S R U R Y I C
M A S T R O R O E O B I R A S Y
M Z C P K E R N B S A A I S L C
I A O R A E R I K T R O N A S L
N R O N H A C K S C L I N U D E
G W L I A S H O E Y M W F E A F
J O G G I N G N I W O R R S A S
```

FIND ALL OF THE FITNESS WORDS IN *THE FITNESS WORD SEARCH!* YOU'LL HAVE TO LOOK UP, DOWN, FORWARD, BACKWARD, AND DIAGONALLY! CROSS THEM OFF THE LIST AS YOU FIND THEM!

FITNESS WORDS:
SWIMMING
JOGGING
ROWING
WEIGHTS
BICYCLE
SAUNA
WORKOUT
AEROBICS
STAIRS
SPA

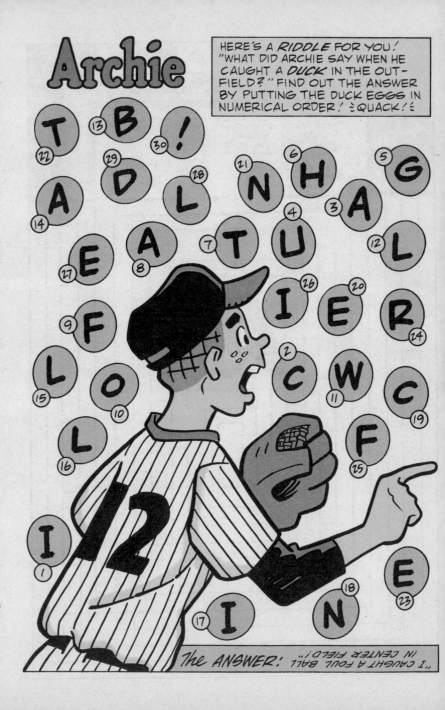

Jughead in Hungry Man!

HOW HUNGRY IS JUGHEAD? USE THE DECODER TO FIND OUT!

C=✿ U=⚡ R=☾ I=✕ M=♥ N=◖ Y=⊖ D=⊛

E=◇ H=◎ G=⬇ S=⊃ O=◯ A=‼ T=# L=☼ !=@

ANSWER:

I'M SO HUNGRY, I COULD EAT A HORSE!

Archie and MR. WEATHERBEE

EXCUSES, EXCUSES

ARCHIE'S LATE FOR SCHOOL AGAIN! WHAT EXCUSE IS HE COMING UP WITH NOW? CROSS OUT THE LETTERS IN THE BOXES CONTAINING AN ODD NUMBER!

4 M	3 T	1 L	6 Y	5 R	11 P	2 C	8 A	9 Y	10 R	15 S	12 W
3 G	16 A	2 S	1 I	4 A	3 I	17 Q	6 B	19 T	8 D	10 U	14 C
10 T	17 L	25 J	4 E	6 D	33 L	19 T	2 B	4 Y	11 P	18 U	7 J
17 Q	20 F	4 O'	15 T	2 S	2 !	13 T	7 X	3 Z	1 S	5 P	5 L

ANSWER: ⟶

MY CAR WAS ABDUCTED BY UFOs!

Archie "Extra Credit"

WHAT DID ARCHIE SAY WHEN VERONICA LENT HIM HER CREDIT CARD?
USING THE DECODER BOX, YOU CAN FIGURE OUT THE MESSAGE BELOW:

DECODER BOX!

Veronica

YES... I'M CUTE!

...AND CHECK OUT THE WORD FIND FOR SOME OTHER CUTE THINGS! LOOK UP, DOWN, FORWARD, BACKWARD AND DIAGONALLY! CHECK THE LIST BELOW.!!

```
L I F L U V E
U T I S T E W A
O N S E L H A
B E R I T S L
A S A I S H E S E I P P U P
S E E H T A C S A P N J A C
E I B E Y R N I C A T K S K
L B I H N E E H A D B R O I
T A N G T H I S E I N N U B
R B A T R C P T H I
U M I O K C A L
T K N S I A Y
```

CUTE LIST:
BUNNIES · TURTLES
KITTENS
PUPPIES · BEARS
BABIES · CHICKS

ARCHIE-GARAGE MESSAGE

ARCHIE TOOK HIS CAR TO THE GARAGE FOR A TUNE-UP AND SAW AN INTERESTING SIGN THERE. FIND OUT WHAT IT SAYS BY BLACKENING OUT THE FOLLOWING LETTERS — B, C, O, F, H, K, L, M, P, Q, U, W AND Y.

S B CLUMPYS
E A S O N
B U Y DUCKY
G
R H L PNGS
W E AS I G
QU L LUCK

Betty SPRING FLOWERS

```
L Z I N N I A A I R T L G E E
I M K C E Y D N V E I U O N Y
L I Y P P O P A Y L O H E N R
Y I R I S S Y L A E B O P A O
      C V I E B L U L
      C N D A I S Y G
      D E N T A L A G
      L C R C I K B N
      O H O U N E R I
      G Y S R U A S N
      I E E B T E C R
      R V T D E I N O
      A T Y N P R O M
      M A A I L H A D
```

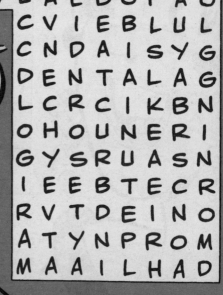

MARIGOLD • DAHLIA • ROSE
LILY • ZINNIA • LILAC
POPPY • PETUNIA • IRIS
MORNING GLORY • DAISY

ARCHIE-GET A HOMER

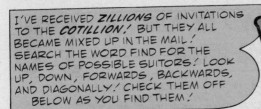

I'VE RECEIVED **ZILLIONS** OF INVITATIONS TO THE **COTILLION!** BUT THEY ALL BECAME MIXED UP IN THE MAIL! SEARCH THE WORD FIND FOR THE NAMES OF POSSIBLE SUITORS! LOOK UP, DOWN, FORWARDS, BACKWARDS, AND DIAGONALLY! CHECK THEM OFF BELOW AS YOU FIND THEM!

L E A H C I M E

```
L E N H O J
L H C A S G
I R O M D A
T H B A R R Y G
R I T E I
C C E E R R
H H I T R R
I A G O I A
E R G N A N
D D E Y N R
S S U R Y R
C L Z Z O G
O O S T I N
T O C Y U S
Y T I P A E T
D V W K A I H
X E R T H U T
D A V I D E L
M M S I R H C
```

FIND THESE NAMES!!
MICHAEL · CHRIS · MARK · DAVID
BILL · SCOTT · JOHN · RICHARD
ARCHIE · REX · BARRY · REGGIE
VICTOR · DAN · PAUL · TONY

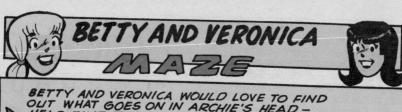

BETTY AND VERONICA WOULD LOVE TO FIND OUT WHAT GOES ON IN ARCHIE'S HEAD – HELP FIND THE PATH THROUGH THE MAZE.

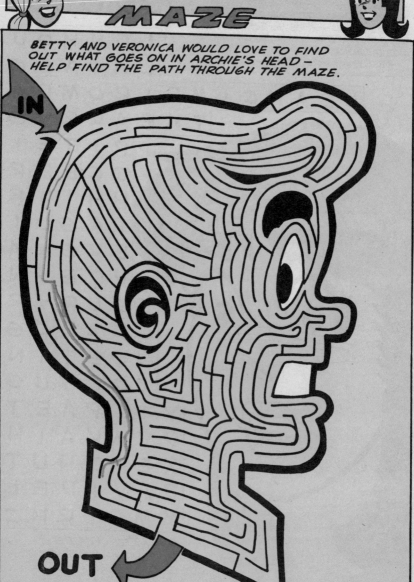

IN

OUT

DILTON'S MONDO
NAME·SEARCH!!

HERE'S A *GREAT PUZZLE!* FIND THE NAMES OF *24 ARCHIE CHARACTERS* IN THE NAME SEARCH!!

THE NAMES ARE LISTED AT THE BOTTOM OF THIS PAGE!!

```
O W K E N F
H E Y R O Y
D A A R O Y
N O N U O N
T T I U S I
A T R H E T
N R B D A I
```

```
M R S V E N S O N E G N I E P T A N C D
H A A E A B L I E R Y D N U R G S S I M
S T L B S A T N V Y T H S R C A T H N C
T G E E H A M O O S E U E I T P E N O T
A O M I T S D S N O S E U O R T A E R S
E D W H A R E A S I T Q I E S N M U E M
L T D C T O S J E P O F V A T E E I V O
K O N R T E O U L O P U R E S H R F R C
H H E A I Y R G J P O C E A I Z L R E E
C H U C K O B H O T A E G D H E E A E G
A N E O R R M E S A V A G L D L H D L D
O E R T O E A A I T I H I I E D T L E I
C W N O T L I D E E B R E H T A E W R M
```

MONDO LIST!! → DILTON·ETHEL·SABRINA·HOT DOG·REGGIE·POP TATE·SALEM·JUGHEAD·MR. WEATHERBEE·ARCHIE·HILDA·VERONICA·JASON·AMBROSE·CHUCK·LEROY·MOOSE·JOSIE·MIDGE·ZELDA·MISS GRUNDY·MR. SVENSON·COACH KLEATS

Jughead IN "I SCREAM for Ice Cream"

YEP, EVERYONE LOVES ICE CREAM, BUT NOT AS MUCH AS FORSYTHE P. JONES!
AND IF THERE'S A NEW FLAVOR OUT, HE'S SURELY ALREADY DISCOVERED
IT! LOOK FOR SOME YUMMY ICE CREAM FLAVORS IN THIS WORD FIND!

```
V  C  R  C  P  Q  Z  P  T  C  M
M  O  C  H  A  A  L  M  O  N  D
O  O  M  U  G  E  L  B  B  U  B
I  K  P  U  X  R  Y  N  O  R  U
H  I  C           T  Y  O  T
C  E  Z           U  C  T  T
A  D  L           D  K  E
S  O  M           T  Y  R
S  U  T           V  R  R
I  G  C           G  O  U
P  H              A  M
L  O              D  C
R  J              T  Y
C  F              R  N
```

WORD LIST · MOCHA ALMOND, PISTACHIO, ROCKY ROAD,
BUBBLE GUM, BUTTER RUM,
COOKIE DOUGH

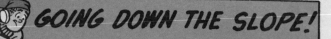

ARCHIE NOTICED AN INTERESTING SIGN AT A SKI LODGE. FIND OUT WHAT IT SAYS BY UNSCRAMBLING THE JUMBLES. HINT: TO HELP YOU WITH THE HARD WORDS, THERE IS A NUMBER GIVING THE POSITION IN THE WORD.

CONATIU—
TEH WALS FO
TRIGAVY
REA TRYLICTS
DRONECEF!

Archie Homework Blues

HOMEWORK, HOMEWORK AND MORE HOMEWORK! FIND OUT WHAT THINGS ARCHIE WOULD RATHER BE DOING THAN HOMEWORK!

```
Q E Z K G N I C N A D
D A T I N G V R P S J
G T Y S I N G I N G L
N I J S H         P
I N A I T
L G E N O
W I O G N
O U X S A
B P
```

REALLY HARD MATH

ANSWERS:

DANCING, EATING,
DATING, KISSING,
BOWLING,
NOTHING,
SINGING!

JUG-SUNRISE FUN-RISE

JUGHEAD HAS SOME ADVICE FOR THOSE WHO HATE TO GET UP IN THE MORNING.

FIND OUT WHAT IT IS BY PUTTING THE NUMBERED LETTERS INTO THE SAME NUMBERED BLANK SPACES.

G E T T I N G   U P   I N   T H E
10 2 9 9 4 12 10   5 11   4 12   9 13 2

M O R N I N G   I S   J U S T   A
14 1 8 12 4 12 10   4 6   16 5 6 9   3

M A T T E R   O F   M I N D
14 3 9 9 2 8   1 15   14 4 12 7

O V E R   M A T T R E S S
1 17 2 8   14 3 9 9 8 2 6 6

1. O	7. D	10. G	16. J
2. E	8. R	11. P	17. V
3. A	9. T	12. N	
4. I		13. H	
5. U		14. M	
6. S		15. F	

Veronica JET Setter

FILL IN THE NAMES OF THESE PLACES VERONICA'S BEEN TO! WHEN COMPLETE, HER MEANS OF TRANSPORTATION WILL BE SHOWN IN THE DARK BOX!

ANSWERS:

① L.A. ② PARIS ③ RIO ④ ALPS
⑤ CHILE ⑥ JAPAN ⑦ NICE ⑧ ROME
SPECIAL WORD: AIRPLANE

WHAT KIND OF ICE CREAM DO YOU WANT IN YOUR ROOT BEER FLOAT? FIND YOUR CHOICES IN THE WORD SEARCH! LOOK UP, DOWN, FORWARD, BACKWARD, AND DIAGONALLY! CHECK THEM OFF THE LIST BELOW AS YOU FIND THEM!
Archie
F S F A L O S D
B T U Y N I U N
V R C R A N K B
H A T K E R A A H R Y E C U
N I N W O E O O T T
E I B C B C L H T
L E O P N I N E
L R L S G I R R
A R A A M E V P
I Y T R A E E E
E C E S L A L C
R P C U C E N A
C P E H H D D L N
M E A T I W L A Y O
P H E P P O L I T I
A R A R T W I T G N
E T A L O C O H C
O O K H I M I M N
ICE CREAM FIND WORDS:
PEPPERMINT * RASPBERRY
BUTTER PECAN * PEACH
CHOCOLATE * STRAWBERRY
VANILLA * CHOCOLATE CHIP

WHAT'S BREWIN'?

SABRINA'S AUNTS ZELDA AND HILDA WANT TO WHIP UP A WITCH'S BREW, BUT THEIR INGREDIENTS ARE A LITTLE MIXED UP! CAN YOU UNSCRAMBLE THE LETTERS TO SEE WHAT EACH ONE IS?

ANSWERS : BAT WINGS , GNATS' EYES , LIZARD'S TAIL , SALT AND PEPPER

Sabrina -The COUNT!-
SEE IF YOU CAN COUNT THE NUMBER OF TIMES SABRINA'S NAME APPEARS BELOW!! BUT, BE CAREFUL, SOMETIMES THEY OVERLAP!!
ANSWER: 21

in LIGHTS OUT!

FILL IN THE BOXES WITH THE CLUES GIVEN! THEN IN THE SPECIAL UP AND DOWN BOX, SEE WHAT REGGIE'S HOPING FOR WHEN HE FIGHTS ARCHIE!

SPECIAL WORD ↓

1. REGGIE IS A BIG ____ !

2. HE THINKS ARCHIE IS A REAL ____ !

3. REGGIE'S GOT THE BIGGEST ONE AROUND !

4. VERONICA CALLED HIM ONE RECENTLY !

5. REGGIE WILL PUT THE ____ ON MIDGE ANYTIME !

6. HE'LL DO THIS IN ANY MIRROR !

7. HE'LL GIVE HIMSELF A ____ AND KISS ANYTIME !

8. HE'S JUST ____ ON HIMSELF !

★

Answers:

SPECIAL WORD: KNOCKOUT
7. HUG 8. STUCK
4. CLOD 5. MAKE 6. LOOK
1. JERK 2. NERD 3. EGO

YOU SPENT *HOW MUCH* ON ACCESSORIES?

MERE POCKET CHANGE, MY DEAR!

UH OH! VERONICA WENT ON ANOTHER ONE OF HER SHOPPING SPREES, AND THIS TIME SHE BOUGHT ACCESSORIES! TRY TO FIND ALL THE ITEMS LISTED BELOW!

SCARF, PURSE, HAT
BELT, EARRINGS, GLOVES, NECKLACE
SOCKS, BRACELET, SUNGLASSES

```
H L Q N O P G P A S B Q N
R T B R A C E L E T A H E
O U S F R A C S O I M X C
M K W Y U O S G C V R Z K
T V X C Q A V N Q T E O L
S W B Z L K G I E L U S A
K O X G J M P R Z S K F C
C P N J S U Y R F M R W E
O U P E R T O A Q V N U K
S A N T K L F E B E L T P
```

Archie in "KISS ME YOU FOOL"

IN THE FOLLOWING WORD SEARCH, FIND ALL THE WORDS THAT DESCRIBE ARCHIE AND BETTY'S RELATIONSHIP!

WORD LIST →

KISSES, DATES, HEARTS, DUO, COUPLE, RELATIONSHIP, HUGS ROMANTIC, LOVING, FRIENDS

YES, FRIENDS! BETTY'S GONE *ARCHIE CRAZY* AGAIN! SEE HOW MANY TIMES YOU CAN FIND THE NAME *ARCHIE* IN THE WORD FIND! LOOK UP, DOWN, FORWARD, BACKWARD AND DIAGONALLY!!

Betty

```
W H E I H C R A L A L T H E A
T Y O S A Y E A M E S A S R E
A N H D I N G I T E I H C R A
A R C H I E A B H H E H J O N
L L V O E A O T U C I A A K S
            E R J R C O
            E A C E N
            I E H I O
            H U I H T
          Y C M E C O
          A R C H R Y
          A U S A T
          D I T F
            F E I
            F I H
          E R E H
          N O C
          G R R
          I R A
```

GOSH, OH, GOLLY!

ANSWER: NINE

PRO-SKATE

HOW DID VERONICA BECOME SUCH A SUPER SKATER? SHE LISTS 3 VERY IMPORTANT REASONS BELOW!

UNSCRAMBLE THEM AND YOU'LL UNDERSTAND!

1. CRATEPIC

2. APCTRIEC

3. RCICETPA

Archie MAD BOY PUZZLE!

BOY, IS ARCHIE MAD! FIND OUT WHAT ELSE HE IS IN THE WORD FIND BELOW! LOOK UP, DOWN, FORWARD, BACKWARD, AND DIAGONALLY! THEN, CHECK YOUR ANSWERS AGAINST THE LIST BELOW!

```
K E U S I A D E G A R T U O
D L M M N I I S N G T S L A
R D I G K N U H U P S E T N
D E R E L O O E U S R I G I
E Y H I I D
T A N R I A
S I U O D M
U F N G S T
G N D S O H
S R O U R C
I E B A E K G
D G N I M U F
```

I'M PEEVED!

MAD BOY WORD LIST!
DISGUSTED · OUTRAGED · FUMING
ANGRY · FURIOUS · UPSET · SORE

Josie's Puzzle

JOSIE AND THE PUSSYCATS ASK YOU TO FIND 17 WORDS THAT PERTAIN TO MUSIC IN THE PUZZLE BELOW.! THE WORDS MAY BE READ FORWARD, BACKWARD UP, DOWN, OR DIAGONALLY.! THE WORDS ARE IN A STRAIGHT LINE AND THEY NEVER SKIP A LETTER.! SOME WORDS OVERLAP AND SOME LETTERS ARE USED MORE THAN ONCE.!

1. ALBUM
2. AMPLIFIER
3. ARRANGEMENT
4. BAND
5. BLUES
6. DEEJAY
7. DRUMMER
8. GIG
9. GROUP
10. GUITAR
11. HARMONY
12. LYRICS
13. MELODY
14. MICROPHONE
15. RECORDING
16. RHYTHM
17. VOCALIST

A	Z	Y	R	E	M	M	U	R	D	X	M
B	L	C	F	A	P	U	O	R	G	E	A
D	E	B	L	U	E	S	K	N	L	R	M
H	B	G	U	H	I	J	I	O	R	G	P
T	A	L	M	M	N	D	D	A	H	U	L
S	N	R	O	P	R	Y	N	X	Y	I	I
I	D	Q	M	O	T	G	V	Z	T	T	F
L	R	S	C	O	E	U	I	W	H	A	I
A	X	E	X	M	N	Z	G	G	M	R	E
C	R	Y	E	G	L	Y	R	I	C	S	R
O	E	N	O	H	P	O	R	C	I	M	Z
V	T	Y	G	V	R	Y	A	J	E	E	D

NOTE SAMPLE WORD "ALBUM"! SCORE A POINT FOR EACH WORD THAT YOU FIND!

TURN PAGE UPSIDE DOWN FOR ANSWERS

ARCHIE-MAKE OR BREAK Puzzle

ARCHIE WANTS YOU TO FIND OUT WHAT EVERYONE MAKES AT THE END OF THE YEAR.

SOLVE THE REBUS BY WRITING THE PICTURE CLUES AND SUBTRACTING OR ADDING *LETTERS* ACCORDING TO THE ARITHMETIC SIGNS!

ANSWER

RESOLUTIONS

JUGHEAD MAZE
FIND YOUR WAY THROUGH THE "JUG" MAZE.

Betty's PIN-UP GIRL

PUZZLE PAGE!

FIND THE TEN "PIN-UP GIRL" WORDS IN THE WORD SEARCH BELOW. THEN CHECK THE ANSWERS AT THE BOTTOM OF THE PAGE!

WOW! LOOK AT BETTY!

```
H D E R C M O N I G M S A
W E D N E S D A Y H O U L
I N E D E R N T G A M M S
S I N B U G I H T G B M E
A S T L E D S U R P S E I
M A R C H S O I H R A R D
O N Y O R A E Y P A E L R
Y U R S F I I F A T I C R
R T E E R R C E R H K E A
A L F S O N M I S S E H D
U K Y S P R I N G N C R N
N E G B A N D A F T U I E
A E T T L K Y L U E P A L
J W A O R U O S T S Z R A
M O N D A Y F R I D A Y C
```

WHAT'S MY SCARIEST THOUGHT?

FIND OUT BY CROSSING OUT ALL THE LETTERS IN BOXES CONTAINING **ODD** NUMBERS! THE ANSWERS ARE BELOW! ...HARUMPHH!

MISTER LODGE

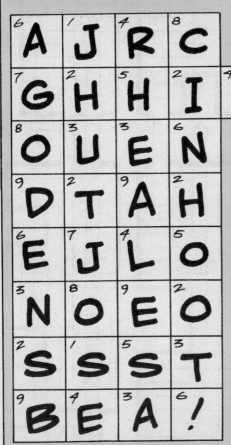

A	J	R	C
G	H	H	I E
O	U	E	N
D	T	A	H
E	J	L	O
N	O	E	O
S	S	S	T
B	E	A	!

THE ANSWER: "ARCHIE ON THE LOOSE!"

ARCHIE MAZE

FIND YOUR WAY THROUGH THE A-R-C-H-I-E MAZE
WITHOUT GETTING TRAPPED IN THE DEAD
ENDS.

IN

OUT

MR. & MRS. **ANDREWS** are **PROUD PARENTS!**

USE THE **DECODER** BELOW TO FIND OUT WHY ARCHIE'S MOM AND DAD ARE SO **HAPPY!!**

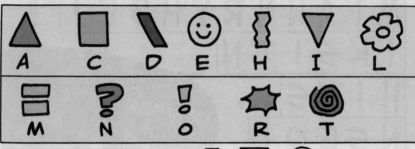

THE ANSWER!

"ARCHIE MADE THE HONOR ROLL!"

Veronica in SHAPE UP!

UNSCRAMBLE THE WORDS BELOW TO DISCOVER SOME OF THE EXERCISES AND EQUIPMENT SHE USES TO STAY IN SHAPE. THEN UNSCRAMBLE THE HIGHLIGHTED LETTERS TO FIND THE ANSWER TO THE QUESTION BELOW.

1. S I B R A O E
2. S H I P U C N
3. L L B B S U M E D
4. N C H U R C E S
5. G G G I O J N
6. L L D A T E R M I

WHAT DOES VERONICA EXERCISE MOST OF ALL?

HER _____ !

THE ANSWERS:
1. AEROBICS 2. CHIN UPS 3. DUMBBELLS 4. CRUNCHES 5. JOGGING 6. TREADMILL CREDIT CARDS!

Archie in OH, MY HEAD!!

ARCHIE ASKS THAT THROBBING QUESTION, "WHAT CAN GIVE YOU A HEADACHE... BESIDES MOOSE'S FIST?" USE THE CODE TO FIND OUT! ANSWERS BELOW!!

					M	↓	◐	¢	↓	#
				#	O	¢	?	$		
*	↓	△	$	☆	O	@	!!			
☺	¢	↑	*	◐	S					
				*	E	◎	◐			

A	◎	M	△
E	$	N	#
G	↑	O	↓
H	*	R	@
I	¢	S	?
K	!!	T	◐
L	☺	W	☆

ANSWERS:

MOTION - NOISE
HOMEWORK
LIGHTS - HEAT

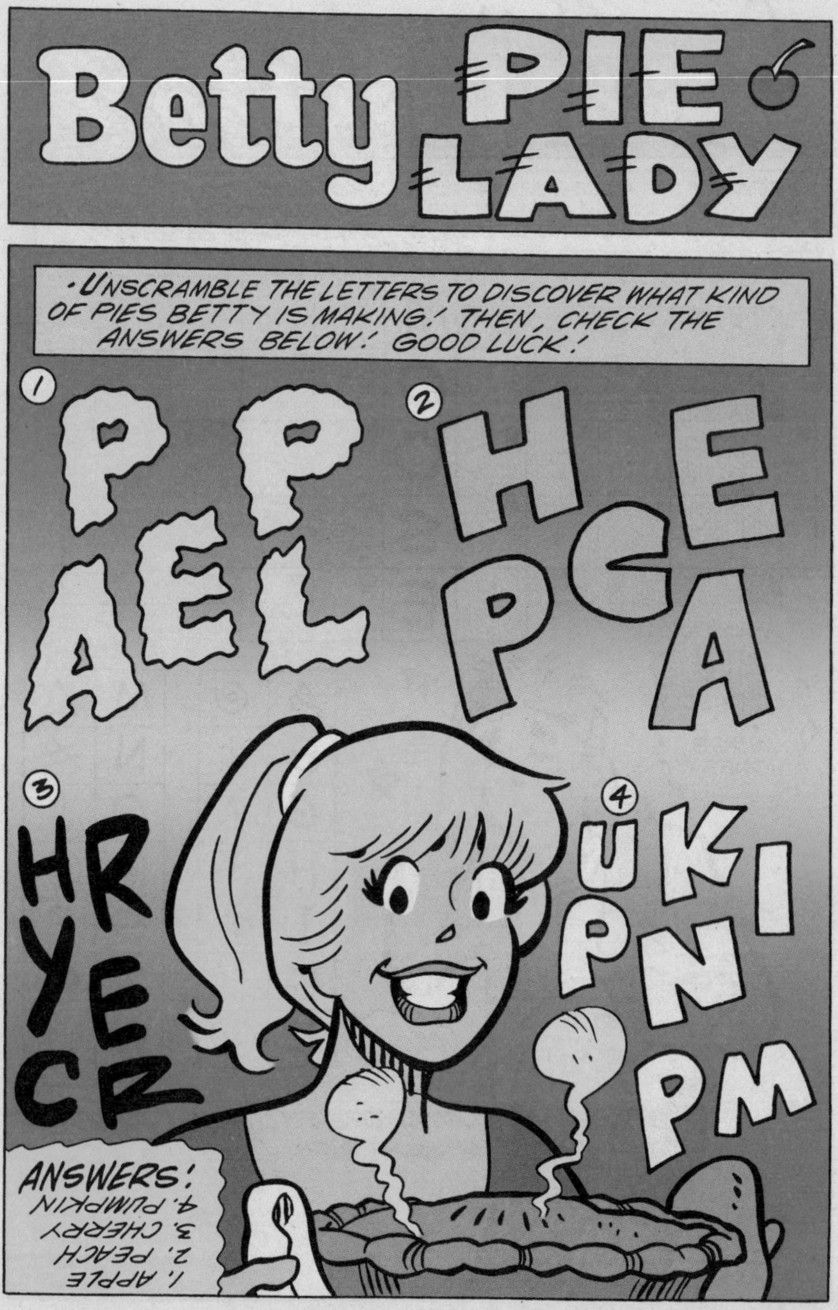
Betty PIE LADY
UNSCRAMBLE THE LETTERS TO DISCOVER WHAT KIND OF PIES BETTY IS MAKING! THEN, CHECK THE ANSWERS BELOW! GOOD LUCK!
1 P P A E L
2 H E P C A
3 H R Y E C R
4 U K I P N P M
ANSWERS!
1. APPLE
2. PEACH
3. CHERRY
4. PUMPKIN

ARCHIE - *OOPS!*

WHAT KIND OF *FALL* MAKES YOU UNCONSCIOUS, BUT DOESN'T HURT YOU?

THE ANSWER WILL APPEAR WHEN YOU BLACKEN THE FOLLOWING LETTERS —
O, B, C, D, M, R, T AND U.

ANSWER

FALLING ASLEEP!

Reggie IN "ONCE IS **NOT** ENOUGH!"

REGGIE CAN'T SEEM TO GET ENOUGH OF HIMSELF! MAYBE THAT'S WHY HIS NAME IS PRINTED OVER AND OVER! COUNT AND SEE IF YOU CAN TELL HOW MANY TIMES IT'S LISTED IN THIS PUZZLE.

```
G R R E R R R R I R
R E G G I E G E R E
R G G R E G G I E G
G G R E G G I E G G
R I E G E I R I G I
R E G G I E         E
E I G I R G         R
G G I E R           G
G G E   G           R
I E O             I G
E R I
```

Answer:

TEN TIMES

Betty — MY BEST FRIEND!

¹N	³C	⁶H	¹I	⁷G	³A	⁸E	¹D	³N
⁵L	¹A	⁶C	³C	⁷K	⁷N	³E	⁷Y	⁷A
⁹E	³T	⁹A	⁴R	³D	⁹N	⁸D	¹I	⁶I
¹N	²A	⁷I	⁹Y	³E	²R	⁷H	³G	¹T
³Y	¹A	³L	¹R	⁷V	¹I	³S	⁴Y	⁷O
¹H	⁵R	¹C	⁹M	⁵A	⁷E	¹I	¹N	³O
¹N	³C	⁷H	¹I	⁷G	³A	⁵E	¹D	³N

The ANSWER:

HER DIARY!

VERONICA STADIUM MAZE

VERONICA WAS TO MEET ARCHIE AT THE BASEBALL STADIUM, BUT SOMEHOW THEY MISSED EACH OTHER.
HELP VERONICA FIND ARCHIE THROUGH THE MAZE.

HOT DOG 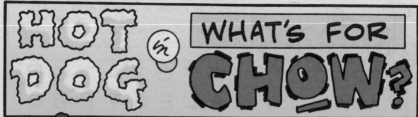 WHAT'S FOR CHOW?

CROSS OUT EVERY OTHER LETTER TO FIND OUT WHAT HOT DOG IS HAVING FOR DINNER TONIGHT!!

S	T	O	S	U	E	P	H
B	P	O	A	N	N	E	I
L	E	I	S	V	U	E	C
					R	K	C
					S	H	S
					I	I	C
					N	K	A
					E	F	N

SCRITCH!

1. SOUPBONE
2. LIVER
3. CHICKEN

Archie's PUZZLE PAGE!

LOST COIN MAZE!!

ARCHIE'S DONE IT AGAIN, GANG! ON THE WAY TO A COIN SHOW, HE DROPPED HIS MOST VALUABLE COIN DOWN THE SEWER DRAIN! HELP ARCHIE FISH IT OUT! WATCH OUT FOR ALL THE OTHER JUNK IN THE DRAIN!!

START!

FINISH!

SHEESH!

MISS GRUNDY HAS HEARD A LOT OF EXCUSES IN HER DAY, BUT THIS ONE FROM ARCHIE REALLY TOPS IT ALL! CROSS OUT ALL THE Gs, Js, Os AND Rs TO UNCOVER HIS LAME EXCUSE!

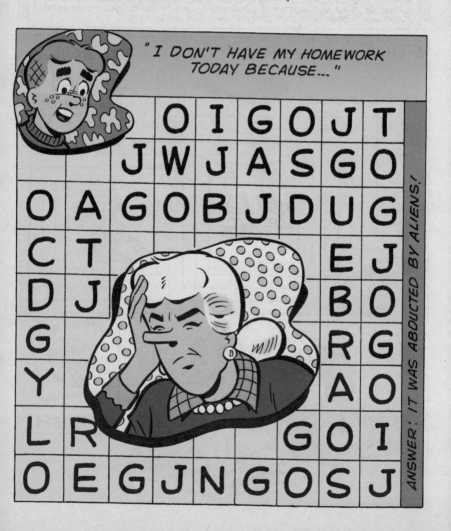

"I DON'T HAVE MY HOMEWORK TODAY BECAUSE...."

ANSWER: IT WAS ABDUCTED BY ALIENS!

Archie's MOM BAG LUNCH
WHAT DID ARCHIE'S MOM PACK FOR HIM IN HIS LUNCH BAG? UNSCRAMBLE THE LETTERS ... OKAY?!
1 YALNOBE
2 RBE ABD
3 PE PE ALP
4 E TUC ELT
The ANSWERS:
1. BALONEY 2. BREAD
3. APPLE 4. LETTUCE

BETTY'S MAZE

FIND YOUR WAY THROUGH THE B-E-T-T-Y MAZE WITHOUT GETTING TRAPPED IN THE DEAD ENDS.

IN

OUT

Veronica "That's Amour"

HOW ABOUT A LITTLE QUIZ IN FRENCH, READERS? SEE IF YOU CAN MATCH UP THE FOLLOWING ENGLISH WORDS WITH THEIR FRENCH COUNTERPARTS.

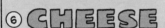

ENGLISH	FRENCH
① LOVE	Ⓐ MAISON
② FRIEND	Ⓑ AMI
③ LIKE	Ⓒ VOITURE
④ CAR	Ⓓ FROMAGE
⑤ HOUSE	Ⓔ AMOUR
⑥ CHEESE	Ⓕ AIME

Answers:

6 - D
5 - A
4 - C
3 - F
2 - B
1 - E

LE DUH!

Archie

...SHOULDER BONES...

...CONNECTED TO THE ARM BONE... --AND SO ON... FIND THE NAMES OF BONES IN THE WORD FIND. LOOK UP, DOWN, FORWARD, BACKWARD AND DIAGONALLY! CHECK THEM OFF BELOW AS YOU FIND THEM.

```
S H O U S
C H D L S
A I L D O
P P O E R
U B H R E O F
L O E B M F L
A N N O U Y E
T E E T H O S
R U L L U K S
P E M R T U R
```

```
S N O N E G O
U D U L N A E
I N I O O S A
D E A S B I R
A R N I R E B
R B R O A N E
          L G T
          L T R
          O O E
          C G V
```

BONES:
VERTEBRAE
SCAPULA
COLLARBONE · SKULL
RADIUS · RIBS · TEETH
HIP BONE · ULNA · HUMERO

Moose "SCHOOL DAZE"

UH-OH! IT LOOKS LIKE MOOSE JUST GOT HIS REPORT CARD! UNSCRAMBLE ALL OF THE SUBJECTS BELOW TO SEE WHICH ONES HE DIDN'T DO SO WELL IN.....

1. DOWO-POSH
2. SIUMC
3. RIS'HOTY
4. NGSILHE
5. CIOLSA-TESIDUS
6. ECISENC
7. TMHA

ANSWERS:

1. WOOD SHOP 2. MUSIC 3. HISTORY 4. ENGLISH 5. SOCIAL-STUDIES 6. SCIENCE 7. MATH

Veronica
STOP STARING AT ME AND UNSCRAMBLE THE LETTERS TO DISCOVER SOME MONTHS OF THE YEAR! --TIME'S A RUNNIN' OUT!!
1 BAURFRYE
2 RILAP
3 STUGAU
4 PTEERESBM
2 3 4 5 6
9 12 13
15 16 19 20
22 23 26 27
The ANSWERS:
1, FEBRUARY
2, APRIL
3, AUGUST
4, SEPTEMBER

Archie (in) SMOOCHFEST

KISSING IS AN ART TO ARCHIE AND THE GIRLS! IN THIS WORD SEARCH, FIND
ALL THE WORDS THAT PERTAIN TO KISSING!

```
C L I P S V R C S M O O C H O B L
R Q I L K E Y G L V R Y S Z M R Y
V C Q I L I P S T I C K P P T E O
I V U T S R Q P O N M L J U K A F
S V W X Y Z N S M A C K I C N T O
E P Y L C O V M Y C A K B H C
    B S Q L K G E N E E M X
          C S P T R T I N
          Q W E M N I
          T N O T B
          X X Z S B
          I D P L
          B L E
          X C S
          I R M
          _ C D
          V Y X
          V S U D
```

WORD LIST:

LIPS, SMOOCH, LIPSTICK, PUCKER,
BREATHMINTS, SMACK, PECK,
NIBBLE!

Betty IN FACE IT!

ONLY 17 AND SHE'S ALREADY FINDING THOSE LITTLE LINES IN HER FACE! UNSCRAMBLE THE FOLLOWING AGING SIGNS BETTY HOPES NOT TO FIND SOON!

1. NKWELRIS

2. (2 WORDS) CEFTWSORE

3. SGBA

4. (2 WORDS) GEILUHNLAS

ANSWERS:

1. WRINKLES
2. CROW'S FEET
3. BAGS (UNDER EYES)
4. LAUGH LINES

ARCHIE·SNOW TRAIL

ARCHIE IS LOOKING FOR VERONICA WHO GOT LOST UP IN THE SNOW-COVERED MOUNTAINS. VERONICA HAS BEEN GOING IN CIRCLES AND LEFT A TRAIL OF FOOTPRINTS IN THE SNOW.

HELP ARCHIE TRACK HER DOWN.

Veronica
UNSCRAMBLE THE WORDS THAT MEAN "WALK" OR "WALKING!" THE ANSWERS ARE GIVEN BELOW!
1 RUT ST
2 TOR LL S
3 AN ERDW
4 TP EN' IP S
5 A TN RE SU
6 UCIT K RN'
The ANSWERS:
1. STRUT 2. STROLL 3. WANDER 4. STEPPIN' 5. SAUNTER 6. TRUCKIN'

Archie

```
N E S N E F D S
T U M N Y G E N
N E R A B I G D I P P E R R A Y
V O V Q A N Y A W Y K L I M A M
G O K I T W I N K L E A D G B E
N I R A C R H I U H S A H D E N
          B E B S U I R I S
            M E N A R A
            R E S I B I
            I   B I R
            C   U L A
            A   R A L
            A   L A O
                  P
```

Star List
MILKY WAY
POLARIS
NOVA
SIRIUS
BIG DIPPER
TWINKLE
NEBULA · SUN

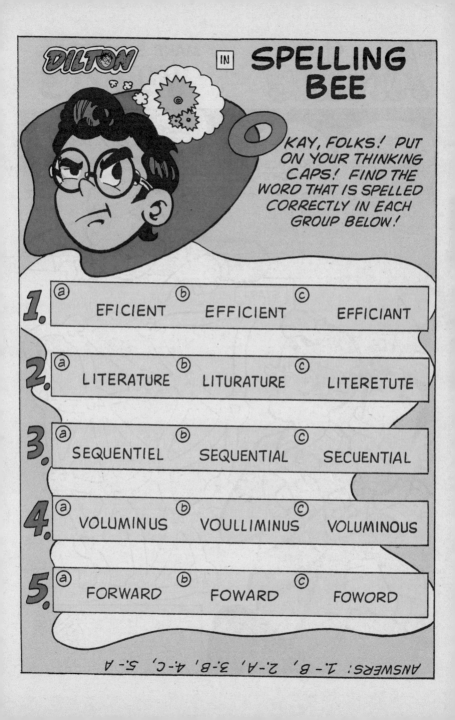

Veronica in "WANNA LIFT?"

AFTER A DAY OF FROLICKING AROUND WITH VERONICA LIKE THIS, ARCHIE'S GOT JUST ONE THING TO SAY TO HER! PUT THE LETTERS IN NUMERICAL ORDER TO SEE WHAT THAT MESSAGE IS!

ANSWER: YOU'RE BREAKING MY BACK!

Betty

BETTY AND ARCHIE'S DATE WAS GOING JUST PERFECTLY UNTIL NOW! FIND OUT WHAT HAPPENED BY CROSSING OUT EVERY OTHER BOX AND READING THE REMAINING LETTERS! THE FIRST ONE IS CROSSED OUT FOR YOU!!

			B	~~T~~	E	R	T	E	T	C	Y
C	S	A	P	A	A	N	R	N	E	E	N
B	T	R	S	Z	C	E	A	P	M	O	E
H	H	O	O	P	M	B	E	G	E	N	A
K	R	C	L	A	Y	H	!	A	S	P	O,
T	N	T	O	A	G	T	O	R	O	E	D
E	N	R	I	N	G	L					
H	H	T	D	K	A	I					
I	S	R	S								
C	T	R	O								
U	N	Y	I								
P	G	Y	H								
C	T	T	!								

THE ANSWER:

"BETTY'S PARENTS CAME HOME EARLY; SO, NO GOODNIGHT KISS TONIGHT!"

Jughead in "SNOW WOE"

JUGHEAD SHOULDN'T HAVE DONE THAT! USE THE FOLLOWING CODE TO FIND OUT WHAT VERONICA IS THINKING RIGHT NOW!

ANSWER:

I HOPE JUGHEAD ENJOYS HIS LAST CHRISTMAS!

HERE I AM ... SINGING AGAIN! DISCOVER WHAT KINDS OF TUNES I LIKE TO BELT OUT BY FINDING THE MUSIC TYPES IN THE WORD SEARCH! LOOK UP, DOWN, FORWARD, BACKWARD, AND DIAGONALLY! CROSS THEM OFF AS YOU FIND THEM! RING-A-DING-DING! ♫

TUNE TYPES:
BALLAD
TORCH
COUNTRY
ROCK
POP
SWING
JAZZ
BOP
RAP

WHAT'S COOKING?

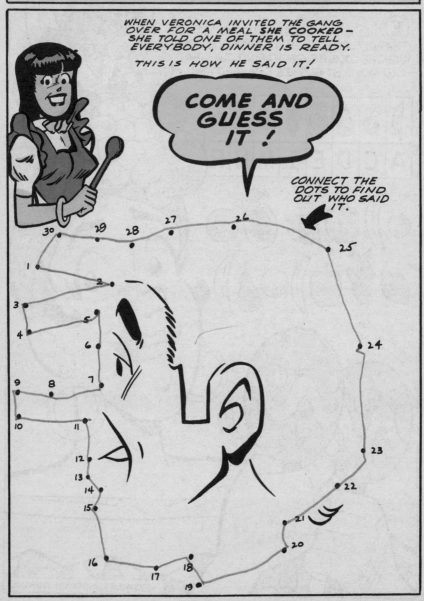

Jughead THROW AFFAIR!

FORE!

```
L L A B T O O F S T Z Y O
Y O F Y D W I L V O N T T
L S R N S D I F Y N E N R
L T I L H J K B X F T E S
A S S L O I N
B H B A T L D
E B E B P U S
S T E W U S
A F T O T Z
B X A N M I
S B G S C W
```

WORD LIST:
BASEBALL · FRISBEE
FOOTBALL · SHOTPUT
SNOWBALL

Reggie in SWEET REVENGE!

REGGIE SABOTAGED ARCHIE SO HE COULDN'T MAKE HIS DATE WITH BETTY! SO WHY IS SHE SMILING? PUT THE LETTERS WITH NUMBERS IN ORDER TO FIND OUT WHAT OUR SWEET GIRL HAS COOKED UP!

Answer:

Archie WORD LADDER PUZZLE

HEY! HOW DO YOU DO THAT?

Is MR. WEATHERBEE RIGHT? CAN YOU *CHANGE ONE LETTER* IN EACH OF THE THREE STEPS TO CHANGE *BALD* TO THE WORD *HAIR*?

1. BALD

2. _ _ _ _

3. _ _ _ _

4. _ _ _ _

5. HAIR

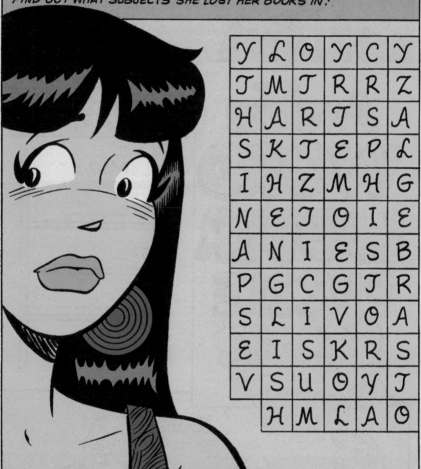

MR. LODGE THE Last STRAW

OH, BOY! WHAT DID ARCHIE DO NOW? PUT THE LETTERS IN NUMERICAL ORDER AND FIND OUT WHAT HE DID!

ANSWER:

HE SAT ON MRS. LODGE'S STRAW HAT!

Archie

```
E E A R C E A R C H I E R I
I A R H I A R C H I E A H C
H C H H A R C H I E
C I C A R C H I E
R R A R C H I E
A R C H I E E A
R R A R C E A E
C I C H I E R I
H E A H I H C H
I R C H I C H C
E R C A R E I R
A R C H I E E A
A R C H I E A E
R R R C H I I
C R C A E H I
H C H H C I
I E I R I H
E A A R C E
```

THE ANSWER: 02

Jughead TOOLS OF THE TRADE!

JUGHEAD TAKES COOKING VERY SERIOUSLY!
TRY TO FIND THE 7 CULINARY INSTRUMENTS
IN THIS TASTY WORD SEARCH!!

```
A S P A T U L A B K
B L E N D E R D R S
C R E T A R G E E I
F I L K N R S G M H
L O E Q W T P J I W
H M R E N I A R T S
```

WORD LIST :

SPATULA ✳ BLENDER
WHISK ✳ GRATER
STRAINER ✳ PEELER
✳ TIMER ✳

Betty AUTO CLASS!

BETTY'S BEEN TAKING AN AUTO REPAIR CLASS! HELP HER FIND THE **10** CAR PARTS IN THE WORD SEARCH! LOOK UP, DOWN, FORWARDS, BACKWARDS, AND DIAGONALLY! CROSS OFF THE WORDS IN THE LIST BELOW AS YOU FIND THEM! GOOD LUCK !!

```
H T L T F A H S K N A R C S T
W O R I N E S E L H E E W E L
H B E M U N E V E S
E E T S A U C A L I
E R L E F R D L I D
L M I B P L N V A L
D I F E I R U E A
B A L G S A O I S
E T H E T I R E
E T E S O H N
W Y N P N H O
S A T A R N E
F C B E L T L
```

FIND 'EM!

CAR PARTS LIST!!
FAN · HEADLIGHT · PISTON
CRANKSHAFT · VALVE · WHEEL
TIRE · FILTER · HOSE · BELT

Archie

```
B H B S Y S T R D S I S L O O
E A C E O Y A E T I F S N L R
U P G R E E N D H G W I R E A
L E E U L I F I T E L O I V N
B C A F L I P E L L O I G Y G
        C A C U D E
        E E P K Y B
        O T N E E R
        C I D H L N
        P H J O L S
        W S N O O
        T O N W C
        H N T R O
        N O K A K
        E W E C C
        N O O N A
        E A H R L
        C O O W B
```

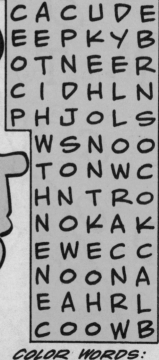

COLOR WORDS:
ORANGE · BROWN · PINK
YELLOW · GREEN · WHITE
RED · BLUE · VIOLET · BLACK

PROF. FLUTESNOOT

FIND THE NAMES OF THE **SCIENCE** WORDS IN THE BLOCK OF LETTERS! LOOK UP, DOWN, FORWARD, BACKWARD AND DIAGONALLY!

```
S E M N A C T
K E A M R A O
A E T R T R N
Y D T O O B N
N R E F P O S
D A R A S N O
T N R E T U P M O C S H R N T W
E T D       N A N A I R U S N
S W         D O U B E S S O
N           L Q L T L A T
U           Y T I V A R G
            B M E G N R A
              E N S
              G O O
              Y T M B
              X O B A
              O R A R
              A P R
          P A I S E R
          N I N R A S R
        O F M S B O Y T E
```

WHERE ARE THEY?

FIND THESE WORDS:
· CARBON · BRAIN · COMPUTER ·
· OXYGEN · GRAVITY ·
· PROTON · QUASAR · MATTER ·
· SUNSPOT ·

Archie in "Young Love"

BETTY WISHES SHE COULD GO EVERYWHERE LIKE THIS, BUT UNFORTUNATELY, SHE CAN'T! WHAT DID BETTY SAY TO ARCHIE TO PROMPT THIS? USE THE DECODER BOX TO FIND OUT!

Answer:

I COULD USE A LITTLE MORNING PICK ME UP!

Betty GOLLY! It's a Herring!

BETTY'S THINKING ABOUT DOING SOME FISHING DURING HER SUMMER VACATION! UNSCRAMBLE THE LETTERS BELOW TO FIND OUT WHAT UNDERWATER GAME SHE'LL BE PURSUING! GOOD LUCK!!

1. TABHILU

2. LUBL EGLI

3. NASMOL

HOLY MACKERAL!

ANSWERS: 1. HALIBUT 2. BLUEGILL 3. SALMON